The Secret Mermaid

The Dark Queen's Revenge

Sue Mongredien

Illustrated by Maria Pearson

For the real Arwen Rich, with lots of love

First published in the UK in 2010 by Usborne Publishing Ltd., Usborne House,
83-85 Saffron Hill, London EC1N 8RT, England. www.usborne.com

A CIP catalogue record for this book is available from the British Library.

JFM MJJASOND/10

ISBN 9781409506409 96100
Printed in Reading, Berkshire, UK.

Contents

The Mermaids of the

Shanti

Molly

Eloise

Leila

Undersea Kingdom

Queen
Luna

Aisha

Iona

Phoebe

Chapter One

Molly Holmes felt very cheerful as she walked along the dark road with her mum. Not only had school broken up that day for the Christmas holidays, but she'd also just had a really fun few hours round at her friend Chloe's house.

"First we played this game where we were detectives and had to rescue Chloe's teddy from the evil Duvet King," Molly told her mum, giggling as she remembered the way Chloe had dramatically flung herself on the bed, pretending to wrestle with her duvet. "Then we made some chocolate brownies with her mum. And then we played a computer game with Chloe's brother before tea. Oh, and look what Chloe lent me!"

She held up the book and her mum peered at it through the gloom. It was early evening but already dark and cold, with just the lamp posts and twinkling stars above to provide any light.

"*Children's Guide to Sea Creatures* by Arwen Rich," her mum read aloud, and she laughed. "I'd have thought you already knew everything there was to know about sea creatures by now, Molls, with all the things your gran's told you."

Molly smiled to herself. It was true that she'd found out all sorts of wonderful facts about sea life since they'd been living in Horseshoe Bay…but she hadn't learned *everything* from her gran! Unknown to her parents, Molly was "the secret mermaid", who sometimes transformed magically into a mermaid at night. Lately she'd been helping the Animal-Keeper mermaids on a very special mission, and she was hoping that Chloe's book might come in handy for her next adventure.

"Well, it's always good to find out new stuff," she said vaguely to her mum now. She didn't add that the main reason she'd wanted to borrow this particular book was because it had

a whole chapter about octopuses – and it was really important to Molly that she found out everything she could about them!

Recently, Carlotta, a bad mermaid who called herself "the Dark Queen", had returned from her banishment and was causing lots of trouble. She had used some powerful magic to capture all the whales, dolphins, penguins, seahorses, turtles and octopuses, shrunk them to tiny sizes and kept them prisoner in secret places around the seas. She had also stripped them of various powers which had left the animals weakened. For instance,

Carlotta had stolen the dolphins' ability to swim extra-fast and the seahorses' ability to camouflage themselves. Nobody was sure why she had done this, but the mermaids suspected she was plotting something terrible.

Molly and the Animal-Keepers had so far managed to track down and set free all of the creatures except the octopuses. During these rescue missions, Molly had been helped by her magical animal charm, which had been given to her by a walrus. While she was wearing the charm, sea creatures would come to her aid if ever she needed help. The charm also had the ability to lend Molly special powers that only sea creatures usually had. She'd been able to keep warm like a penguin, leap out of the water like a whale and even protect herself with a kind of armour like a turtle's shell. It had been amazing!

And now I'll be able to find out what special abilities octopuses have, Molly thought, tucking the book under her arm as she walked along. *After all, if I'm going to tackle the Dark Queen, I'll need all the help I can get!*

Once they were home, Molly settled down with Chloe's book in the living room. To Molly's surprise, it turned out that octopuses were absolutely *astonishing* creatures, and extremely clever. "Wow," she said to herself as she read. "Cool!" Then she looked up. "Hey, Mum, did you know that octopuses can defend themselves by squirting black ink into the water?"

Her mum was trying to read Toby, Molly's baby brother, a bedtime story, although Toby seemed more intent on chewing the book than actually looking at the pictures. "Squirting ink?" she echoed. "What do you mean?"

"Well, if another creature is trying to catch the octopus – a shark, say – then the octopus squirts out a cloud of black ink and the water turns black. Then he can get away quick, while the shark can't see," Molly replied. "Genius!"

Molly's gran, who was leafing through the newspaper at the other end of the sofa, chuckled. "They're wonderful creatures," she said. "They can get through the tiniest spaces too, because they have no bones. It's quite something to see them squirming through a small gap between rocks. In aquariums, I mean, obviously."

Molly and her gran exchanged a meaningful look which luckily went unnoticed by Molly's mum, who was still trying to take the board book out of Toby's mouth. Gran, of course, knew all about Molly's mermaid adventures, because she'd been the one who'd started them off in the first place, giving Molly the special conch shell necklace which magically took her into the mermaid world. Gran had been the secret mermaid too, once upon a time, although they weren't allowed to swap stories about their experiences. The Merqueen herself, Queen Luna, had told them that being a secret mermaid meant just that – you had to keep it to yourself, or the magic would stop.

Molly turned back to her book, and the very next thing she read was about octopuses' flexibility. "Wow," she murmured. "It says here that even a big octopus can squeeze through a hole the size of a ten-pence piece. That is amazing!" She read on eagerly, fascinated by this unusual creature. "Oh, and there's a bit here about how being clever and good at squeezing through small gaps makes them brilliant escape artists." She giggled. "It says they often manage to break out of their tanks in aquariums, and break *in* to other tanks, to eat the fish there!"

"Goodness!" Molly's mum said, laughing as well. "I bet that keeps the aquarium staff on their toes."

Molly read on, her mind racing. She couldn't help wondering which of the octopuses' powers the Dark Queen would have wanted to steal – and whether or not she had succeeded. Still, looking on the bright side, Molly would be able to ask her animal charm to lend her all these powers too, wouldn't she? It would certainly make for another exciting mermaid adventure, next time she found herself in the Undersea Kingdom!

I hope it's soon, Molly thought, crossing her fingers secretly behind the book. *And I hope I'm not already too late to rescue the octopuses!*

Chapter Two

That night, after Molly had said goodnight to her parents and Gran, she made sure her special necklace was in its usual place, on her bedside table. The pale piece of conch shell gleamed in the darkness and she reached out to touch it, and the silver animal charm, with her fingertips. "Please let the magic work tonight," she whispered. She didn't become a mermaid every night, unfortunately, however much she would have liked to. She knew that she had to wait for the magic to happen all on its own.

Shutting her eyes, she rolled over, pulling the covers right up around her neck. It was cold that night, and she could feel the freezing sea air whispering through her draughty bedroom windows. She tossed and turned for a while, trying to get comfortable, and then, just as she was starting to think she was *never* going to fall asleep, she sensed a sudden brightness in the room, even through her closed eyes, and opened them at once.

Yes! The conch shell on her necklace was shining through the darkness, with pink sparkly magic streaming out from it.

That only meant one thing…she was about to have a mermaid adventure!

She shut her eyes again hurriedly and the magic took hold in the very next second. As always, Molly felt as if she were falling very fast and very far, as if a giant hand had picked her up and then dropped her. Then a warm, tingly feeling spread throughout her body and she heard gentle splashing sounds. Now she could feel the weightlessness of being in water, and opened her eyes immediately to see that, once again, she was a mermaid, with her own glittering green tail. Hooray!

Molly was in a coral reef this time, and she gazed around in delight at all the different coloured fish and other creatures swimming past her. There were gorgeous striped clownfish whizzing by in a blur of orange, and a spiny pufferfish cruising sedately along with a haughty expression on its face. Elsewhere, there were crabs scuttling across the seabed, green and blue plants rippling like beckoning fingers... Oh, and there was another mermaid swimming towards her, smiling and waving!

Molly recognized Iona at once – she had met her along with all the other Animal-Keeper mermaids in Queen Luna's palace courtyard when the animals had first gone missing. Iona had long brown hair, tied up in a ponytail and pale skin dotted with freckles. She had a wide smile and beautiful violet eyes, and a silver octopus charm which dangled from a chain around her neck.

"Hello there," Molly said as she approached. "Nice to see you again! Any news on the octopuses?"

"Hi," Iona replied. "I don't have any definite news, although I've come here to investigate something that a couple of jellyfish told me about. There's a 'magic walking cowrie shell' in this reef apparently, which sounds very unusual. I couldn't help wondering if it had something to do with the missing octopuses. Want to help me check it out?"

"A magic walking cowrie shell?" Molly repeated in surprise. "That does sound weird. Where is it supposed to be?"

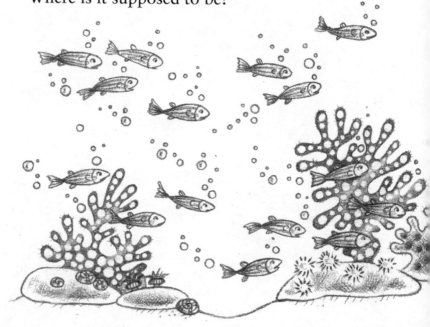

"Near the seaweed jungle at the edge of the reef, they said," Iona replied. "It's this way. Follow me."

Molly and Iona swam through the bustling reef, past colourful anemones, sea urchins and a whole school of cute zebra fish.

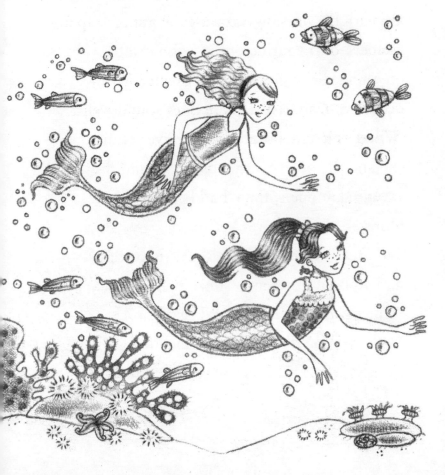

At last, they came to an area where a mass of dark green seaweed grew tall and thick, the leaves swaying in the gentle current and making a soft swishing sound.

"We need to be careful," Molly said in a low voice as they slowed down. "The Dark Queen isn't working alone. If the shell *is* connected to your octopuses, you can bet anything she'll have left guards nearby to defend it. Dangerous guards."

She shivered at the thought. Every time she and the other mermaids had found the captured animals, there had been horrible monster-like creatures lurking nearby, which had attacked the mermaids. The monsters had all been different – some made of rock, some of coral, some of mud, sand or ice. Molly couldn't help her gaze flicking uneasily to the tangled branches of the coral reef

behind her, double-checking that they weren't
actually monster arms waiting to grab her at
any moment.

Iona looked serious. "Leila and Shanti told
me about those monsters," she said quietly.
"We'll be on our guard. Come on. Let's hunt
for this cowrie shell – very carefully."

The mermaids swam further along the edge
of the reef. They hadn't gone far when they both
caught sight of something very peculiar ahead,
and stopped still to stare at it. There, lurching
jerkily along the seabed, was a brown-spotted,
egg-shaped shell. As they watched, it rocked
from side to side and moved across the sand.
It really did look as if it were walking!

Iona's eyes were very wide. "There's the cowrie shell," she said. "But I've never seen a cowrie move like that before! Cowries are sea snails," she explained, "so they travel very slowly – not jerking sideways like that one."

"Could it be a hermit crab?" Molly ventured. She knew that they made their homes in different shells.

Iona shook her head. "If it was a hermit crab, we'd see its legs sticking out the bottom." She grinned. "No legs there. Come on, let's have a proper look. I'm curious."

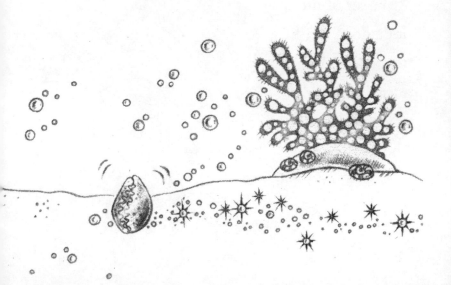

She and Molly swam over to the shell and Iona picked it up. Usually, cowrie shells had an opening at the bottom, but this one had been sealed closed with what looked like a thick, glassy substance. Molly's heart thumped as, through it, she could see thousands of tiny, speck-like creatures, moving in a mass together.

"Do you see them?" she asked Iona excitedly.

"Yes," said Iona, peering closely. "Masses of titchy little dots...with tentacles!" Her face lit up. "It's my octopuses!" she whooped. "We've found them!"

"Brilliant," Molly said with a big smile. Then she glanced nervously behind her, scared that a monster was about to rear up nearby and snatch the shell back. She braced herself for the attack, knowing it was sure to come soon. She had to be ready for the monsters!

Iona giggled, and Molly looked around. The tiny octopuses had all moved to the same side of the shell together and their force made the shell tip up in Iona's hands.

"*That's* how they were moving it along," Iona realized. "They must have been leaning from one side of the shell to the other, all in unison." She laughed again. "They are so clever, these guys, they really are. Even at this tiny size, they still instinctively know what to do."

"I was just reading last night about what great escape artists octopuses are," Molly smiled. "Looks like they're making a pretty good escape attempt right now!"

"They've certainly managed to escape from wherever the Dark Queen hid the shell," Iona said. "So now we just need to get them out of here." She beamed. "Oh, this is wonderful! I've been so worried about them."

Molly couldn't help checking over her shoulder again. "We have to watch out for monsters, though," she said cautiously. "The Dark Queen is sure to have left some of them guarding the octopuses. They're probably watching us right now!"

Chapter Three

Iona bent over the shell. "What's the best way to get these little guys out, do you think?"

Molly thought hard. "Well, octopuses are very flexible, aren't they?" she said. "So hopefully we only need to make a tiny hole in the shell and they'll be able to squeeze through it. Maybe if we—"

She broke off as she suddenly heard a faint clicking sound coming from the shell. She and

Iona peered through the solid glassy covering and saw that all the tiny octopuses had gathered at the bottom of the shell and seemed to be hurling themselves at its wall.

Click, click, click. Tap, tap, tap.

"What *are* they doing?" Iona muttered.

Molly suddenly remembered that when she and Shanti, another mermaid, had found the missing turtles, they'd been shrunk and hidden inside a clutch of eggs. Molly and Shanti had encouraged the tiny turtles to bash the insides of the shells with their strong, clawed flippers, and the eggs had eventually broken. Could the octopuses possibly be attempting the same thing now?

"I think maybe they're trying to break out all by themselves," she said to Iona.

Iona's eyes widened. "They are, aren't they?" she laughed. "They must be using their beaks to try and shatter the shell!"

Molly knew from reading Chloe's book that octopuses were completely squidgy and boneless apart from their strong beaks, which were sharp and curved, rather like parrots' beaks. Click, click, click, they went against the shell now. Molly grinned. "The octopuses don't need our help at all," she laughed. "They worked together to move the shell out of its hiding place, wherever that was. And now they've thought of a way to escape from the shell itself!"

"They've cracked it!" Iona suddenly cried, pointing out a small line that had appeared on the surface of the cowrie shell. Her eyes sparkled with admiration for the clever creatures. "And now it should be short work for them to squeeze through there.

An easy job for my octopuses, you watch!"

Both mermaids waited for the octopuses to squirm through the narrow opening in the shell – but nothing happened. "Oh," said Iona in surprise. "That's odd." She peered into the shell. "I can see some of them are certainly *trying* to squeeze through," she said after a moment, "but they don't seem able to." She bit her lip. "I hope they're okay."

"Can we help them out?" Molly wondered. "Can we make the crack bigger somehow?" She looked around the seabed for inspiration. If she had been at home, she'd have used a needle or pin to poke through the crack and try to pick it open. Was there something similar they could use here?

Her eye fell on a sea urchin nearby. It was green with purple-tipped spines. Would it be willing to help? She hesitated. The only time she'd met a sea urchin before was when she'd

been helping one of the
Shell-Keeper mermaids,
Delphi, look for her piece of
the magic conch shell. That sea
urchin had been incredibly bad-tempered and
aggressive, even threatening to jab them with its
spines. But she had to try asking, for the sake of
the poor octopuses.

"I've got an idea," she said to Iona and swam over to the sea urchin. "Excuse me," she said politely. "I was wondering if you might help us."

The sea urchin's spines rippled for a moment, then it inched nearer and looked at Molly. "Oh!" it said in a sweet, shy voice. "Oh my goodness. Is that really the animal charm you're wearing?"

Molly smiled in relief. This already seemed a *much* nicer sea urchin than the last one she'd met.

"Yes, it is," she replied. "And if you don't mind, I think your beautiful spines would be the perfect thing to help us."

"Mind?" the sea urchin echoed, quivering in excitement. "I don't mind at all. I would be honoured to help a mermaid with the animal charm. Tell me what you want me to do."

Molly beckoned to Iona, who brought the cowrie shell over to them. Then she explained her plan. "If you could just push a couple of spines against this crack, I think you might be able to widen it slightly," she said to the friendly sea urchin. "But please be careful. There are some living creatures trapped in the shell and we'd hate to hurt any of them."

They didn't need to worry. The octopuses seemed able to hear and understand perfectly, for they immediately backed away from the crack in the shell to keep safe.

The sea urchin wiggled right up to the shell and then slowly and carefully fitted the sharp pointed tips of three spines into the small crack. Then she began to press herself against the crack with all her might.

Molly held her breath as she watched. She hoped this would work! The sea urchin had to push hard enough to split the shell a little wider, but not so hard that she accidentally speared any tiny octopuses. "Keep going," Molly murmured encouragingly. "Just a bit more..."

The sea urchin was starting to turn red, she was pushing so hard. And then, all of a sudden... Crack! The split in the shell widened...and all the teeny octopuses came streaming out!

"Thank goodness!" Iona cheered. "Oh, you did it, well done!"

"Yes, well done," Molly said, scooping up the sea urchin so that the octopuses wouldn't tear their tentacles on her spines. "And thank you very much!"

As the octopuses escaped into the seawater, they began to grow bigger and bigger and bigger, until they were back to their usual size. There was such an amazing range of colours and sizes, Molly thought, gazing at them all in delight. There were the stunning-looking blue-ringed octopuses, which were poisonous according to Chloe's book. There were gigantic pinky-orange octopuses with amazing suckers all over their tentacles. And there were brown and red octopuses, shooting themselves backwards through the water at great speeds.

"Goodness," breathed the sea urchin, her eyes boggling at the vast number of octopuses that now floated around them. "When you said there were living creatures in that shell, I never expected *this*!"

"They are so cool, aren't they?" Molly smiled. "And it's all thanks to you that we got them out!"

Iona was hugging a particularly enormous orange octopus which had wrapped all its tentacles around her. "It's good to see you again," she cried happily.

"It's good to...ow...see you too," the octopus replied.

"Are you okay?" Iona asked, pulling away in concern. "Does something hurt?"

"Not exactly," the octopus said, waggling a tentacle. "Ow. I'm just a bit achy."

Molly could hear lots of the other octopuses saying the same thing. They all seemed to be grumbling about feeling sore and stiff. Then she saw one octopus trying to wriggle between a couple of large rocks – and being surprised when it couldn't get through. "What's wrong with me?" it asked, rubbing its head with one end of a tentacle. "Why can't I fit through that gap?"

Iona was looking less happy and more worried by the second. "Oh dear," she said. "They don't seem as flexible as usual. That must be why they couldn't squeeze out of the crack in the shell."

"I think the Dark Queen must have taken
that power from them," Molly realized. "That
means she'll have the ability to squeeze through
tiny gaps herself now but...why would she want
to do that?"

Iona's forehead creased in a frown. "I know
one place she's been desperate to get into for a
long time," she said. "The Undersea Kingdom,
and the Merqueen's palace!"

The two mermaids stared at each other in
horror. If Iona was right, then Queen Luna was
in great danger. "Come on," Molly said urgently.
"We've got to go to the palace at once!"

Chapter Four

As Molly and Iona swam towards the palace together, followed by the octopuses, the ocean was alarmingly quiet. The fish and other sea creatures Molly had seen earlier all seemed to have vanished.

Suddenly they spotted a lone basking shark, who looked relieved to see Molly and Iona.

"There you are!" he cried. "I've been searching for you two. There's an emergency at the Merqueen's palace. We've got to hurry!"

"An emergency? What do you mean?" Iona asked.

"The Dark Queen's back," the shark gabbled, his tail twitching behind him as he spoke. "She and this whole army of...*monsters* have attacked the Merqueen's palace. Queen Luna's trapped inside."

"Oh no," Molly groaned. This was terrible news. She and the other mermaids had guessed

the Dark Queen was plotting something big, and this was clearly it. She swallowed nervously. If the Dark Queen had all the horrible monsters with her, that was a fearsome army. No wonder there hadn't been any of them guarding the octopuses – they had all been summoned to help with the attack!

"Is the Merqueen managing to keep Carlotta back?" Iona asked, her face very pale.

"Yes," the shark replied. "So far Her Majesty's powerful magic is holding Carlotta at bay. But she's not going to be able to keep that up for ever."

"Let's hurry to help her, then," Molly said at once. "The sooner we get there, the better."

They swam on as quickly as possible, with the basking shark filling them in on more details as they went. According to him, all the sea creatures were on their way to the palace as well. Even though many of them, including him, were scared of the Dark Queen and her evil magic, they all wanted to help defend the Undersea Kingdom and the Merqueen.

"What I don't understand is why she's attacked now," Molly said as they surged through the water. "I mean, why didn't she do it earlier, when she first stole the animals' powers?"

"I don't know," Iona replied, her expression grim. "It may be that she wanted to build up a strong army first, rather than go in alone. I bet she's been quietly creating more and more monsters until she felt that their strength, combined with her new powers, was an unbeatable force."

Molly nodded, feeling afraid. The Dark Queen would be a truly terrifying opponent with all the incredible powers she'd stolen from the animals. She'd be an expert in camouflage like the seahorses, a super-fast swimmer like the dolphins and able to withstand extreme cold like the penguins. Not only that but she'd also have armour-style protection like the turtles, super-flexibility like the octopuses and a brilliant sense of direction like the whales. Oh yes, and she also had a huge army of monsters at her beck and call.

"How on earth are we going to stop her?" Molly asked, hoping she didn't sound as despairing as she felt.

There was silence for a few moments, then Iona spoke. "We need to weaken her if we're

going to stand a chance of victory," she replied.
"Between us mermaids, we've got some pretty
useful magic, but against her strength…" She
looked doubtful. "I just don't know, Molly."

They swam on, through the gates of the
Undersea Kingdom, which had been forced
open and swung loosely in the current.

Molly's pulse raced at the sight. Usually the gates were locked tight shut, and only mermaids could open them with special keys. But somehow or other the Dark Queen had found a way in.

Through they went now, with the basking shark, and the octopuses still swimming behind them.

Once they reached the Merqueen's palace, they were greeted by a scene of battle. Hordes of monsters made of rock, sand, ice and coral were scaling the palace walls, while the Dark Queen was making her way towards the palace doors, shouting a string of horrible-sounding enchantments, obviously trying to use her magic to break them open. The Merqueen and Princess Silva were both gazing out of an upstairs window inside the palace, the Merqueen with a protective arm around her daughter, who looked absolutely terrified. Poor Silva had been enchanted and captured by the Dark Queen before – she knew just how wicked Carlotta could be.

The Merqueen had her eyes fixed on the Dark Queen and her lips were moving as if she too were murmuring magic spells to counter the Dark Queen's enchantments, and keep the palace secure.

Various mermaids were trying to stop the
Dark Queen from reaching the palace doors,
but she was clearly using her armour power
because magic spells were bouncing straight
off her in bright flashes of colour, sizzling and
spluttering uselessly in the water. The whales
tried to muscle her out of the way but she
merely pointed a bony finger at them and a

powerful blast of magic shot out from it, freezing the water around them solid, so that they couldn't move.

A gang of swordfish tried to jab Carlotta with their sharp jaws, but with another blast of magic, she conjured up a thick forest of seaweed around them which was so dense and tangled, it seemed impossible to escape from.

Molly and Iona swam quickly towards the
other five Animal-Keeper mermaids who were
huddled together, deep in conversation. "Hi,"
Iona panted. "We came as soon as we could.
What's been happening?"

"It's been awful," Eloise said miserably.
"Everyone's been trying to stop her, but she's so
powerful now that nothing works. The jellyfish
swarmed at her, hoping to sting her but she used
her magic to hurl them away against the walls."

"The dolphins tried mobbing her, but she held them back with her armour power," Aisha put in. "We can't think of what to try next – and it can only be a matter of time before she breaks into the palace."

As they spoke, a group of octopuses launched themselves at the Dark Queen but she held up a hand and streams of cold blue magic spiralled from her palm, whirling the octopuses up together so that their tentacles became tangled in knots.

She had almost reached the palace doors now, and gave a scornful laugh, jeering up at the Merqueen. "Pathetic!" she yelled. "Utterly pathetic. Is that the best you and your rabble can do? You might as well give in now because nothing is going to stop me. I won't rest until I'm inside that palace and sitting on the throne. And then *you'll* be banished to the ends of the oceans, just as you tried to banish *me*!"

"You'll never defeat our queen," Phoebe yelled in defiance. "And you'll never defeat us!"

The Dark Queen laughed. "That's where you're wrong," she taunted. "Your stupid spells won't work on me this time, I'm afraid. Mermaid magic is *very* overrated these days. Animal magic is much more impressive!" She cackled. "You can't keep me out of this palace now that I'm as flexible as an octopus. I'll be able to squeeze right through the keyhole. Watch this!"

Iona gasped in alarm and Molly felt a lurch inside. The Dark Queen had tried to overthrow the Merqueen before, by enslaving animals to attack the mermaids. Molly knew she would stop at nothing to get what she wanted – control over the oceans. Molly and the mermaids had to prevent the Dark Queen from getting into the palace. It was now or never!

Chapter Five

"We've got to stop her!" Shanti cried. "Quick – somebody think of something!"

"If we could just steal back the sea creatures' powers, she'd be much weaker," Molly said, thinking fast. "The turtles said she'd stored the animal powers in a small bottle – look, there it is, tied around her waist. If we could get that back…"

Leila didn't look convinced. "Yes, but how?

We don't have a hope of getting close enough to take it from her. You've seen that armour power she's using – nobody can get near her."

"*I* might," Molly replied staunchly. "I can camouflage myself using the animal charm, remember, and…"

"But how will you get past the magic that's holding everyone else back?" Leila asked.

Molly stared at the Dark Queen. She was concentrating very hard on pushing her hand straight at the keyhole of the palace door, using her octopus powers to squeeze it thinner and thinner, as if her bones were softening…

Then Molly noticed something. The shimmering line of armour power that had surrounded the Dark Queen had vanished.

"She's unprotected," Molly whispered. "Maybe she can only use one power at a time, just like I can with the animal charm. Now's my chance!"

Iona still looked worried. "It's very brave of you, Molly, but I don't know if we should risk it," she said. "It would be very dangerous for you to try such a thing alone."

"But what else can we do?" Molly asked. "I can't think of a better plan, can you?"

Iona fell silent and Molly's heart thumped. She didn't want to show the other mermaids how terrified she felt at the prospect of sneaking up to the Dark Queen on her own and trying to steal back the animal powers. Deep down she wished with all her heart that one of the others *would* come up with a better plan – would think of a safe, easy way to get rid of the Dark Queen once and for all without the risk of anyone getting hurt. But she knew that wasn't about to happen.

"We've got no choice!" she said firmly, as the Dark Queen's hand went right through the keyhole. Molly clutched her animal charm tightly.

"I want to be camouflaged, like a seahorse!" she whispered.

The charm felt hot between her fingers and a hologram of a seahorse appeared on its smooth surface. Then Molly felt herself tingle all over, and glanced down to see that the charm's amazing magic was working again – she had turned exactly the same shade of blue as the water surrounding her and looked completely invisible.

"Be careful," warned Phoebe.

"And good luck," added Shanti.

"Thanks," Molly said, and took a deep breath. Then she swam silently through the water towards the Dark Queen, who was still squeezing herself through the keyhole of the palace door. She'd got one of her arms completely through now and was pushing her head against the keyhole.

Molly felt sick as, with a revolting squelching
sound, the Dark Queen's head began to squish
down in size until the top of it was able to slither
through the small hole like a snake. *Gross!* Molly
thought, edging closer still.

The monsters were still
clambering up the palace
walls and Molly's heart
pounded as she saw them.
There were so many of them,
and they looked determined
to get inside. Some of the
coral-monsters were bashing
at the windows with their
hard knobbly hands, while
the mud-monsters were
leaving dirty, oozing trails of
mud all over the gleaming
white walls.

Molly swam closer to the Dark Queen. There was a small corked bottle hanging from a rope around her middle. According to the wise old turtle who'd originally told Molly about this, the magical animal powers were in the form of a vapour, like a gas, inside this bottle. Hopefully, Molly just needed to pull out the cork stopper and release the powers again. Well, there was only one way to find out.

She reached towards the bottle, her heart hammering even harder. She had never been this close to the Dark Queen before and she felt terrified at the thought of the evil mermaid unleashing a stream of powerful magic her way. But she had to do this – and the sooner the better!

Molly grabbed the bottle and tugged at the cork stopper. It didn't move. She pulled on it a little harder…and accidentally yanked at the rope around Carlotta.

To her horror,
she felt the Dark
Queen stiffen in
alarm. "Get
away from me,
whoever you
are!" she yelled,
dragging herself
out of the keyhole
again, with the same
horrible squelch. Her eyes
glittered with a cold, furious
light, and Molly felt chilled to the
bone. She was sure the Dark Queen could see
right through her camouflage! What was she
going to do now?

Terrified, Molly went blank for a moment,
but luckily Iona had spotted what was
happening. "Octopuses! Help her! Ink the

Dark Queen!" she yelled.

And then – thank goodness! – a whole mass of octopuses swirled up to them, squirting out great clouds of black ink everywhere. The water turned black, and the Dark Queen gave a cry as they were plunged into darkness, blinded by the inky mist that the octopuses had made. Molly fumbled wildly for the little bottle, her fingers slipping on the smooth glass. Once she had hold of it, she pulled with all her might on the cork stopper. But nothing happened. Had the Dark Queen sealed it with an enchantment?

"Get off that bottle!" she heard the Dark Queen scream, and a cold hand grabbed her wrist in the darkness, its long, talon-like nails scratching Molly's skin.

Molly was so frightened she could hardly breathe, but knew she had to hang on to the bottle. She had to rip that cork out if she was ever going to stop Carlotta! She gave one last tug, heaving at it with all her might, as the Dark Queen scrabbled to stop her. And then... Yes! The cork came away from the bottle, and out streamed a bright green vapour, glittering with dazzling magical lights. The vapour was so powerful and bright that it cut straight through the black ink and began shooting all around the water. It broke into six different trails – one that went straight to the octopuses, and others that went to the whales, dolphins, turtles, seahorses and penguins.

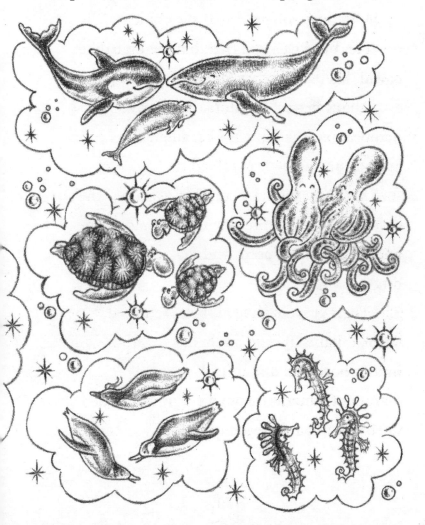

As the inky mist cleared completely, Molly saw that every single one of those creatures glowed the same bright glittering green for a few seconds, and then cries of excitement went up from them all.

"Hey! My shell's turned hard!" a turtle called, his toothless mouth open in a big grin.

"That's better! I'm not so stiff now," an octopus exclaimed, wiggling all eight tentacles at once in glee.

"And we can swim super-fast again!" the dolphins cheered, proving it by zipping back and forth at top speed, and making everyone dizzy.

"Their powers have all been returned," Aisha cried, clapping her hands together with joy. "Oh, this is wonderful!"

A choking cry of rage went up from the Dark Queen, and Molly tried to dive away – but

Carlotta was not going to let her go so easily.
She tightened her grip on Molly's wrist so hard,
Molly thought her bones would be crushed.

"How dare you take my powers!" she screamed
in fury. "Monsters – I need you!"

Molly knew she was invisible to the Dark
Queen – the seahorse camouflage was still
working so Carlotta couldn't see her – but

Molly could see Carlotta, and it was the most terrifying sight. Her mouth was foaming with anger, her eyes gleamed with icy rage and her whole body seemed to be bristling.

The monsters didn't need telling twice. They leaped from the palace walls and thundered across the seabed towards their mistress, their yellow eyes glowing horribly. What would she order them to do? Surely Molly had no chance against them?

Chapter Six

Molly struggled to get away but the Dark Queen held on tight. "No, you don't," she snarled. "You're my prisoner now."

"Help!" shouted Molly. "Help!" And then, thank goodness, she heard Shanti.

"Protect yourself, Molly!" Shanti was yelling urgently. "Use your armour!"

Of course! With her free hand, Molly managed to grab her animal charm. "Give me armour," she gabbled. "Please – I need armour like a turtle!"

The silver charm became hot again and a turtle hologram appeared on its silver surface. Molly's body tingled as the magic took hold, and the Dark Queen gave a sudden cry of surprise when she was forced away by the enchanted armour that now protected Molly.

Using the armour power meant that her camouflage had vanished and Molly had become visible again. Some of the coral monsters threw stones at her, until they realized there was no point – the missiles just bounced off Molly's powerful armour.

Molly swam quickly back to her Animal-Keeper friends, who had taken up defensive positions in front of the palace. Phoebe, who was nearest to her, gave her a hug.

"Well done, Molly. You were amazing."

Just then, a window up in the palace was flung open, and the Merqueen appeared. "It's over, Carlotta," she said severely. "You haven't won – and you never will."

Carlotta definitely seemed weakened by losing her animal powers. She had been swaying in the water, paler suddenly and older-looking, but at Queen Luna's words, she scowled. "Oh yes, I will," she spat. "Don't forget I still have my army. Together we are stronger than you!"

The monsters roared in agreement, several of them hurling missiles up at the Merqueen. The rocks and pebbles bounced off the walls perilously close to her face, and Molly held her breath.

"But you will never be stronger than the mermaids combined," the Merqueen replied calmly, as lumps of rock crashed against the walls around her. She turned her gaze to the mermaids and animals who were still clustered outside the palace. "Well fought, my friends," she said to them. "You did well." Her eye fell upon Molly and she smiled.

"You all showed great courage – but now we need to work together with one last surge of mermaid magic to destroy Carlotta's army. Are you with me?"

"Yes!" replied the mermaids, shouting as one, Molly included.

Queen Luna raised her hand. "Carlotta, it's time to say goodbye to the army you created from evil magic, for evil purposes," she said. She had to shout to be heard over the din of the monsters below. "Mermaids, take hold of any magical items you own, feel the strength from your own good hearts, and wish, wish, wish!"

The Animal-Keeper mermaids all took hold of the silver pendants they wore around their necks. Around them, other mermaids clutched shell rings and bracelets too. Molly's hand went straight to her special necklace, her fingers closing around the magic conch shell and the silver animal charm.

"Wish, wish, wish!" the Merqueen chanted, louder than ever.

I'm wishing, I'm wishing, Molly thought, summoning up every last bit of magical strength from her necklace. *I wish the monsters were gone!*

The water around the mermaids began to pulse with golden lights – faint at first, then growing stronger and brighter.

"Keep wishing!" the Merqueen commanded.
"The mermaid magic is working!"

Thousands of golden lights sparkled through
the seawater now, dancing, spiralling, joining
together in thick, bright streaks that rushed
towards Carlotta and her monsters.

"What's happening to the monsters?" Iona
asked. "Look!"

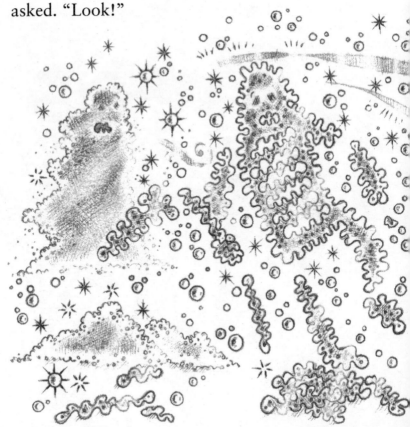

Molly stared in amazement. As the golden sparkles touched them, the yellow lights went out of the monsters' eyes, and they began crumpling lifelessly to the seabed, one after another, like dominoes toppling. Within moments, their bodies were just lumps of mud, sand and coral, as if they'd never been there at all.

The Dark Queen, too, had collapsed to her knees and was clutching her head.

"Help me," she groaned weakly. "Help me."

"Help *you*? After what you've done? You've got to be kidding," Iona cried scornfully.

The palace doors burst open then, and out swam Queen Luna herself, her face forbidding. Silence fell as she swam over to Carlotta and glared at her. "You're a disgrace to mermaids," the Merqueen said coldly. "You thought nothing of our animal friends when you robbed them

of their special powers, you thought only of yourself and your desire for power. You can't just cheat your way into ruling the oceans, you know – you can create all the monsters you like, but you'll never be able to control the Undersea Kingdom through fear alone. There has to be respect – respect for the sea creatures with whom we share the ocean waters, and respect for your fellow mermaids."

The Dark Queen said nothing, but Molly thought she noticed her top lip curling in a sneer.

"I'm sending you to a secure prison cave, where you'll spend the rest of your life," Queen Luna went on. "And guess who I'll be asking to guard you, and make sure you never escape? Our octopus friends, of course. They know all about escaping – and they'll ensure you never get out of there. Take her away!"

The sea creatures didn't need telling twice! A ferocious-looking killer whale scooped up the Dark Queen with its blunt nose and tossed her onto its back. Then, with an escort of octopuses on either side, it glided away from view.

With the Dark Queen safely gone, the Merqueen smiled, looking much more like her usual self, and swam over to the Animal-Keeper mermaids and Molly. "Well done, all of you," she said warmly. "Not only have you worked together to find and set free your missing animals but you've also helped to defeat the Dark Queen again. Molly, my wonderful secret mermaid, special thanks are due to you. Once again, you've shown tremendous courage and quick thinking – we are lucky to have you on our side."

Molly ducked her head in shy pride. "I was glad to help," she said honestly. "I love being the secret mermaid!"

"That's good to hear," Queen Luna said, hugging her. "And now I think this calls for a special celebration. Come, one and all!" she cried, smiling out at all the mermaids

and sea creatures who were gathered there. "You came to my rescue and I am deeply grateful. You are all invited into the palace where a special banquet will be prepared. This is a wonderful night, and we must celebrate!"

Cheers rang out around the water as everyone followed the Merqueen through the palace doors. The whales sang happily, the dolphins frolicked and the seahorses kept changing colour with excitement. Soon afterwards, a wonderful feast was set out on a vast coral table, decorated with mother-of-pearl and sparkling jewels, and Molly was invited to sit with the Merqueen and Princess Silva in special golden chairs at the head of the table.

"Three cheers for friendship and courage!" Queen Luna declared. "Hip hip…"

"Hooray!" the mermaids cheered, so loudly that the sound echoed around the banqueting hall. Molly didn't think she'd ever felt so happy and proud.

Molly wished she could stay at the party all night, but after a while she felt the usual tugging sensation inside her, which meant it was time to go back to her own world. She just had time to hug her mermaid friends goodbye before the sensation grew stronger and stronger, and the Merqueen's palace began to blur before her eyes.

"Come back and see us soon!" Queen Luna called. "And thank you once again, Secret Mermaid!"

Then, before Molly could reply, she was back in her own bed, and the magic was over for another time. She opened her eyes slowly, not wanting her adventure to end. So much had happened this time, what with rescuing the octopuses, defeating the Dark Queen and celebrating her imprisonment with a special party. What a night!

She rubbed her eyes and wriggled into a sitting position, yawning and smiling at the same time. Then, as she looked around her bedroom, she noticed something on her bedside table that hadn't been there the night before. Next to her shell necklace was a pretty bracelet strung with gleaming white pearls. Either Father Christmas had come early, or this was a surprise gift from the mermaids!

She picked it up carefully, running a thumb gently along the polished pearls. Light shone from each bead, and they felt cool and

smooth to the touch. It was so beautiful, and oh, she just felt so happy. The sea creatures had had their powers returned to them and were back to their normal selves, the Dark Queen was gone, and here in her world, Christmas was just around the corner.

Molly put the bracelet around her wrist and fastened its tiny golden clasp. *It's almost the end of a brilliant year*, she thought with a smile, as she heard the waves crashing in against the bay outside. *And I can't wait to find out what mermaid adventures I'll have next year!*

The End

To find out more
about Molly and all her
mermaid friends, and have
some magical ocean fun,
check out

www.thesecretmermaid.co.uk

For more enchanting adventures
log on to

www.fiction.usborne.com

Collect all of Molly's magical mermaid adventures

Enchanted Shell ○ 9780746096154
Molly is amazed to discover that she is the secret mermaid!

Seaside Adventure ○ 9780746096161
Ella and Molly must trap an angry killer whale before recovering Ella's shell.

Underwater Magic ○ 9780746096178
Can Molly win back Delphi's shell from a grumpy sea urchin?

Reef Rescue ○ 9780746096192
Molly and Coral face a swarm of jellyfish to find Coral's shell.

Deep Trouble ○ 9780746096185
Pearl's shell is guarded by sea snakes in a rumbling undersea volcano...

Return of the Dark Queen ○ 9780746096208
Molly must face the Dark Queen to complete the magical conch.

Seahorse SOS ○ 9781409506324
Molly joins in the search for Eloise's missing seahorses.

Dolphin Danger ○ 9781409506331
Molly and Aisha can hear the dolphins' faint calls – but where are they?

Penguin Peril ○ 9781409506348
Could the Dark Queen be behind the disappearance of the penguins?

Turtle Trouble ○ 9781409506355
Scary monsters guard the turtles that Molly and Shanti have come to set free.

Whale Rescue ○ 9781409506393
Molly must save both the trapped whales and her friend, Leila.

The Dark Queen's Revenge ○ 9781409506409
The Dark Queen is back – but can Molly help to end her vile plans?